POKÉMON™

Charizard, Go!

Adapted by Tracey West

SCHOLASTIC INC.
New York   Toronto   London   Auckland   Sydney
Mexico City   New Delhi   Hong Kong

W9-BNK-496

ISBN 0-439-15421-9

12 11 10 9 8 7 6 5 4   0 1 2 3 4 5 6/0

Printed in the U.S.A.

First Scholastic printing, February 2000

Ash's Biggest Match

"You can do it, Ash!"

"We love you, Ash!"

The crowd cheered for Ash Ketchum. The ten-year-old Pokémon trainer squinted into the bright stadium lights. Fans waved and held up signs with his name on them.

Ash wanted to pinch himself. It all felt like a dream. He had worked so hard to get here — to the Pokémon League championships on the Indigo Plateau. He just had to win this battle and his dream would come

true. Ash would finally become a member of the Pokémon League.

The Pokémon League. Every Pokémon trainer wanted to become a member. To become a Pokémon Master, you had to catch one of each kind of Pokémon in the world. And you had to be a member of the Pokémon League.

Getting into the league wasn't easy. First, you had to battle eight Gym Leaders and earn a badge from each of their gyms. Then you had to compete against six other trainers at the Annual Pokémon League Tournament, and beat them all.

Ash had earned his eight badges. He had beaten four trainers at the tournament. Now he was about to fight his fifth battle.

Everyone important to Ash watched from the stands. His friends, Misty and Brock. His mom. And Professor Oak, the Pokémon expert who had given Ash his very first Pokémon, Pikachu, and started him on his Pokémon journey.

Ash's opponent, Richie, faced Ash across the stadium. Richie smiled at Ash, but Ash kept a look of determination on his face.

He liked Richie. Ash and the outgoing, brown-haired boy had become friends during the tournament. But friendship wasn't going to stand in Ash's way. Ash knew he had to battle to win.

The announcer's voice blared through the night air. "The fifth round of the Pokémon League Indigo Conference is about to begin!"

Richie held out a red-and-white Poké Ball.

Pokémon trainers sometimes liked to give their Pokémon nicknames. Richie had nicknames for all his Pokémon.

"Happy! You're up!" Richie yelled.

He threw the Poké Ball in his hand.

The ball opened and a Pokémon that looked like a large butterfly flew out — a Butterfree.

"Squirtle, I choose you!" Ash cried. Ash threw a Poké Ball, and a Pokémon that looked like a cute turtle appeared in a flash of white light.

With a nod from Richie, Happy flew at

Squirtle and slammed into its body. Squirtle responded by shooting a powerful blast of water out of its mouth. Happy countered with another tackle. Squirtle picked itself up and shot another powerful spray of water at Happy.

"Both Pokémon are making a solid attack," the announcer said. "They're very evenly matched."

"Happy, Sleep Powder!" Richie commanded.

The Butterfree began to flap its wings. A shimmering gold powder filled the air around Happy. The powder floated down and covered Squirtle.

Squirtle's eyes started to close. It began to rock back and forth.

Bam! Squirtle fell backward.

"Whoa! Butterfree's Sleep Powder Attack has put Squirtle to sleep," the announcer shouted.

Ash ran to Squirtle's side. Squirtle couldn't be out — not yet.

"Wake up, Squirtle!" Ash pleaded. "Open your eyes!"

Squirtle didn't move.

A judge in a blue uniform stepped onto the field. "Squirtle is unable to battle! Butterfree wins!"

Ash cringed. He held out a Poké Ball and recalled Squirtle.

I can't believe Squirtle lost, Ash thought. *Richie's a good trainer. He used his Butterfree well.*

"At the end of this difficult battle, Butterfree emerges victorious," the announcer said. "What Pokémon will Ash choose next?"

Ash wondered the same thing himself. He had to make a careful choice. In this competition, he and Richie were allowed to use three Pokémon each. The trainer whose three Pokémon fainted first would lose. The winning trainer would go on to the next round of battle. The losing trainer would have to wait a whole year for the next championship.

With Squirtle out, Ash could only choose two more Pokémon. Ash thought about the strategies he'd learned. Butterfree was a Flying Pokémon. Maybe he could use another Flying Pokémon against it. . . .

"Pikachu!"

Startled, Ash looked out on the battle area. His Electric Pokémon, Pikachu, was running out onto the field.

The little yellow Pokémon crashed into Richie's Butterfree with all its might.

"That decides it!" the announcer said excitedly. "Pikachu will be Ash's next Pokémon. It's started the battle with a Double Edge Attack!"

Happy looked angry. The Butterfree flew at Pikachu, scooping up the Pokémon onto its back. They flew high in the air.

Happy lurched and lunged, trying to

throw Pikachu to the ground below.

Pikachu clung on with all its might. Tiny electric sparks flew from its red cheeks.

"Pikachuuu!" cried the lightning mouse.

The air filled with a blast of yellow electric light. The shock coursed through Happy's body.

"It's Pikachu's Thunderbolt Attack!" Ash cried.

The Butterfree plummeted to the ground. Pikachu jumped off and landed on its feet.

Happy crashed into the turf.

"No! Happy!" Richie cried.

"Butterfree can no longer battle," said the announcer. "Pikachu wins!"

Ash looked up at the scoreboard. Richie had two Pokémon left to fight with. Ash had one more he could choose if Pikachu lost.

Ash knew that Pikachu had to hang in there if he had any chance of winning.

"Your Pikachu is really something, Ash," Richie said. "But I know a bit about Pikachu myself. Zippo, it's up to you!"

Richie threw another Poké Ball, and a small, orange-red Pokémon appeared. A Charmander. A Fire Pokémon, Charmander had a flame on its tail and could fight with powerful attacks, such as Rage and Flamethrower.

Ash's palms began to sweat. A Charmander could be a strong opponent.

Zippo opened its mouth and shot a blast of blazing fire at Pikachu. Pikachu just barely dodged the attack.

Zippo wasn't discouraged. The

Charmander aimed blast after blast at Pikachu. Pikachu ran around the battle area, trying to dodge each fiery assault.

"Pikachu is hard-pressed by Zippo's Flamethrower!" the announcer said. "Pikachu is managing to stay out of the way, but for how long?"

Pikachu looked exhausted. Its body was scorched by Zippo's flame.

Pikachu began to reel back and forth. It couldn't run anymore.

"Pikachu!" Ash cried.

Zippo blasted Pikachu with a powerful flame. Then the Charmander lowered its head and ran right at the lightning mouse.

"Uh-oh! Here comes Charmander's Tackle!" said the announcer.

Zippo smacked into Pikachu with a fierce head butt. The impact knocked Pikachu on its back.

Pikachu fainted!

"Pikachu is unable to battle," said the judge. "Charmander is the winner!"

Ash's heart sank. Pikachu was his best Pokémon. Now he was down to one Pokémon. That Pokémon would have to be strong enough to defeat Zippo and Richie's third Pokémon, too.

He could choose Bulbasaur. Bulbasaur was a great fighter.

But Ash knew that Grass Pokémon like Bulbasaur were weak against Fire Types like Zippo.

11

That left only one choice . . .

"I choose Charizard!" Ash yelled, holding up a new Poké Ball.

Misty yelled from the sidelines, "Ash, are you crazy? Charizard doesn't listen to you!"

"You can't win with Charizard!" yelled Brock.

You can't win with Charizard. Maybe Brock was right. Training Charizard was one of Ash's biggest challenges. But Charizard was a super powerful, high-level Pokémon. And it listened to him *sometimes.* If he could control Charizard during the battle, he would beat Richie for sure.

Ash stared at the Poké Ball. What should he do?

He thought back to the experiences he and Charizard had had together, back to when it all began. . . .

2

Charmander, the Stray Pokémon

Ash had only been on his Pokémon journey for a few weeks when he first met Charmander, the Pokémon that would later evolve into his Charizard.

Ash, Misty, Brock, and Pikachu were walking to Vermilion City. Tall trees bordered the dirt road. A large rock jutted out into the path up ahead.

"What's that?" Misty asked, pointing to the top of the rock.

Ash looked. A small, orange-red Pokémon reclined on top of the rock. It looked like a lizard, with a round head and body. A tiny flame burned weakly at the end of its long tail.

Ash took out Dexter, his Pokédex, the small computer that held information about all kinds of Pokémon.

"Charmander, a Fire Pokémon," Dexter said. "A flame burns on the tip of its tail from birth. It is said that a Charmander dies if its flame ever goes out."

"It would be cool to catch a Fire Pokémon," Ash said. He took out a Poké Ball. "I'll have Pikachu battle it and weaken it. Then I'll capture it."

Brock stepped in front of Charmander. "Hold on there, Ash," Brock said. "See how weak its flame is? This Charmander is in no shape to battle."

Ash nodded. "I guess you're right."

Misty looked at a map. "There's a

Pokémon Center just down the road. If we take it there, it can get help."

Ash held out an open Poké Ball. "Come with us, little guy. You'll feel better in no time."

Charmander stubbornly shook its head.

"Why won't it come with us?" Ash asked.

Pikachu climbed up on the rock.

"Pika pika pi?" Pikachu asked.

"Charmander char char," the Pokémon replied weakly.

Pikachu jumped off the rock. It moved its hands wildly. *"Pikachu! Pika pika pika!"* Pikachu said.

Ash understood. "Pikachu says that Charmander's waiting for somebody to come and get it."

Brock sighed. "If it's waiting for somebody, I guess we'd better leave it," he said.

Ash and his team left Charmander and walked down the road. A brisk breeze blew up, and storm clouds darkened the sky overhead. A light rain began to fall.

"I hope that Charmander is all right," Brock said, looking behind him.

Up ahead, they saw a large log cabin in the woods.

"The Pokémon Center!" Misty cried.

They entered the Pokémon Center and sat down in a small booth. Misty got them all soup from the snack counter. They were hungrily eating their soup when they heard a loud voice from across the room.

"I can't believe you left that Charmander on that rock, Damian."

The friends turned around, startled. A group of teenage boys was sitting in a booth, talking. One of the boys had blue hair and wore a pink shirt and leather pants. He was laughing pretty hard.

"That Charmander is so stupid!" Damian said. "That thing was so weak it couldn't beat any opponents. I kept trying to ditch it, but it always followed me. I finally got rid of it by promising I'd come back for it. It's probably still waiting for me!"

Brock looked angry. He got up, walked over to Damian, and picked him up by his shirt collar. Ash, Misty, and Pikachu followed.

"That Charmander is still waiting for you!" Brock said. "Go and get it now!"

"That's right," Ash joined in. "If its flame goes out, it'll die."

Damian pushed Brock away. "What I do is none of your business!" he said. "If you're so worried about that Charmander, then go get it yourself! I don't care what happens to it."

Damian motioned to his friends. "Let's get out of here." They pushed past Ash and out the door.

"What kind of Pokémon trainer abandons his Pokémon?" Ash called out after them.

Brock put a hand on his shoulder. "Let it go, Ash. We've got more important things to worry about."

"Like saving that Charmander!" Misty said.

The friends ran out into the storm. The rain was coming down pretty hard now. Up ahead, they could see the Charmander huddled on the rock, its flame protected only by a small leaf.

A flock of Flying Pokémon called Spearow was attacking the weakened Pokémon.

"Hey, cut it out!" Ash yelled. He threw a rock at the Spearow. The Spearow left Charmander — and attacked Ash.

"Pikachu!" Pikachu cried. It tensed its body, and sent a huge electric shock into the flock of Flying Pokémon.

The Spearow shrieked and scattered into the trees.

"Good work!" Ash said.

Brock climbed up onto the rock. He covered Charmander with his jacket. The Pokémon was too weak to resist. Its flame was so small, it looked like it would burn out any minute.

"I'll protect the flame!" Ash said. As Brock ran down the road carrying Charmander, Ash made sure the flame was covered from the wind and rain.

It seemed like forever before they burst into the Pokémon Center. They rushed Charmander up to Nurse Joy, who took care of all the Pokémon that were brought into the center.

"Please take care of this Charmander!" Brock said, almost out of breath.

"Its flame is almost out!" Ash cried.

Nurse Joy took Charmander from Brock. "You should be ashamed of yourselves," she scolded. "How could you let it get so weak?"

"It's not our fault!" Ash protested. "Damian abandoned it."

Nurse Joy shook her head. "That's terrible. I'll do my best to help it," she said, and whisked Charmander into the hospital room.

19

Ash, Brock, Misty, and Pikachu waited for what seemed like hours for news of Charmander. The clock ticked by slowly.

Please, Charmander, Ash thought. *Please keep your flame burning.*

Finally, Nurse Joy emerged from the room.

She smiled.

"Charmander's recovering," she said. "It should be fine by morning!"

Ash breathed a sigh of relief.

"Thank you so much," he said.

Misty yawned. "We might as well get some sleep," she said.

Ash, Brock, and Pikachu nodded sleepily. They took sleeping bags out of their

knapsacks and stretched out on the couches in the lounge.

All night, Ash dreamed of running through the storm with Charmander. He ran and ran and ran, but he couldn't seem to get to the Pokémon Center.

Ash woke with a start. Sun was streaming through the Pokémon Center's windows.

Everything is all right, Ash thought. *Charmander is all right. I'll be able to see it this morning.*

But everything wasn't all right.

Brock ran into the lounge.

"It's Charmander!" Brock said. "Charmander's missing from the recovery room!"

3

charmander's choice

"Charmander isn't anywhere in the Pokémon Center," Ash said. "We've turned this place upside down."

Ash sighed. "I bet it went back to that rock to wait for Damian," he said. "But I thought Charmander understood that *we* cared about it."

"Don't you see?" Brock said. "Charmander knew that we cared. But it's still loyal to its trainer. That's why it went back."

Misty yawned and stretched. "There's

nothing we can do. We might as well get back on the road to Vermilion City."

Ash and Brock reluctantly agreed. They grabbed a quick breakfast, packed their knapsacks, and headed out onto the path.

"I wish we weren't leaving Charmander behind," Ash said as they walked.

"We did everything we could, Ash," Misty said. "Besides, there will be lots of Pokémon to catch once we get to Vermilion City."

"You're right," Ash said, cheering up a little. "I'll catch so many Poké — whoa!"

Ash felt his feet slip beneath him. He was falling.

Ash crashed to the ground. He looked around. Brock and Misty were sprawled on the ground next to him. They had fallen through some kind of hole.

"Pika?" Pikachu looked down at them from the top of the hole. Somehow the Electric Pokémon had escaped the fall.

"We're all right, Pikachu!" Ash called up.

Misty stood, brushing dirt off her legs. "It looks like we've fallen into some kind of trap!" she said.

"Oh, you've fallen into our trap, all right!"

Ash looked up. A teenage girl with red hair stared down at him with an evil grin on her face. It was Jessie, one member of a trio of Pokémon thieves called Team Rocket. A teenage boy stood next to her — her partner, James. And between them was Meowth, their talking Pokémon.

Instead of their usual red-and-white uniforms, Team Rocket wore blue rubber suits that covered them from head to toe.

"Our plan is working beautifully," James said. "And now to capture you, Pikachu!"

Ash watched helplessly from the pit as James lunged for Pikachu.

Pikachu faced Team Rocket and hurled an electric blast right at them.

The blast fizzled as soon as it hit their blue suits.

"These suits are Pika-proof!" Meowth bragged. "Rubber won't conduct electricity."

Panicked, Pikachu turned and ran. James pulled out a large weapon that looked like a big tube.

"Time to try out our Anti-Pikachu

Rubber Balloon Bazooka!" James said.

James pulled the trigger on the bottom of the tube. A huge, blue rubber balloon poured out of the tube's end. The balloon flew toward Pikachu.

Pikachu ran as fast as it could. But the balloon was faster. It engulfed Pikachu, trapping the Pokémon inside.

"Pikachu!" Pikachu shot angry sparks from its cheeks. Nothing happened.

"You won't escape this time!" Jessie cackled.

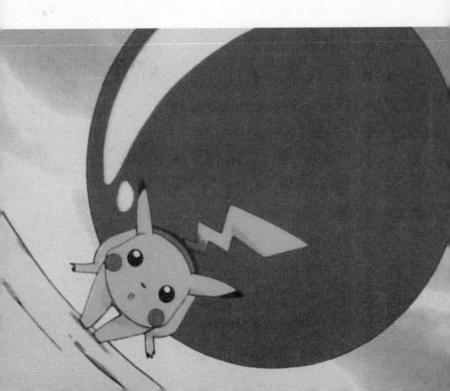

Ash tried to climb out of the hole. It was just too deep. He couldn't get a grip on the soft dirt walls.

It looked like Team Rocket really had Pikachu this time!

Then a small voice filled the air.

"Char!"

It was Charmander!

"Charmander char char!" Charmander told Team Rocket.

"Who's this pip-squeak?" asked Jessie.

"And what's it saying?" James asked.

Meowth understood Charmander. "It's ordering you to give Pikachu back to those guys right now!"

Jessie sneered. "It's got to be kidding!"

James laughed. "Step aside, you little firebug. We haven't got time to play with you."

An angry look crossed Charmander's face. Charmander opened its mouth wide.

A powerful red flame shot from Charmander's mouth.

Team Rocket was scorched!

"Yow!" Jessie and James cried.

"Let's get out of here!" yelled Meowth.

Team Rocket ran off, dropping the balloon that held Pikachu. The balloon popped. Pikachu was free!

Ash, Brock, and Misty finally pulled their way out of the hole. Ash hugged Pikachu.

"Thanks for the help, Charmander!" Brock said.

Misty smiled. "Charmander knew we cared! That's why it's here!"

Ash and Pikachu faced Charmander.

"Charmander, how about joining up with us?" Ash asked. "I'm afraid . . . I think your trainer's not coming back."

Suddenly, Damian emerged from the woods!

"Hey, Charmander," he said. "I've been looking all over for you."

Ash was shocked. "Damian? What are you doing here?"

"I came back for Charmander. Just like I promised," Damian said.

Ash could tell he was lying.

"What are you up to, Damian?" he asked.

Damian ignored him. "Come on, Charmander. Let's go."

Charmander looked at Damian. It looked at Ash. It didn't know what to do.

"Damian, you bragged about how you abandoned Charmander! Why do you want it now?" Ash challenged him.

"It's a good thing I abandoned it! I toughened it up. Besides, what's wrong with dumping off a weak Pokémon?" Damian asked.

29

"Char!" Charmander said in a shocked voice.

"I wasn't gonna come back for it," Damian continued. "But then I saw it make toast of those guys back there. It's pretty strong now. I could use it. And the best thing is, I didn't have to raise it myself!"

"That's terrible!" Misty said angrily. She turned to Charmander. "You see? He doesn't care about you. He just wants you to win matches!"

"Charmander, please come with us," Ash begged.

Charmander looked at Ash. But it didn't move.

"Charmander, return!" Damian commanded. He threw a Poké Ball at Charmander.

The ball flew at Charmander — and Charmander used its tail to knock the ball right back at Damian!

Angrily, Damian held up a batch of Poké Balls. Before he could throw any, Charmander hit him with a blast of fire.

Damian yelped and ran back into the

30

woods. "Who wants a stupid Pokémon like you anyway?" he called behind him.

"Way to go, Charmander!" Brock said.

Ash ran up and hugged Charmander. "You can stay with us, if you want. I promise to raise you to become a great Pokémon."

Charmander smiled and nodded.

"Way to go, Ash," Misty said. "You got a new Pokémon — and a new friend!"

4

From charmander to charmeleon

When Ash found Charmander, he really *had* found a great Pokémon. Whenever Ash called on Charmander to battle, Charmander obeyed. The Fire Pokémon was always ready with a Rage Attack or a Flamethrower Attack to take down its opponent.

Like the time Ash faced a gang of Pokémon trainers on bicycles called the Bridge Bike Gang. Ash and his friends were trying to cross a bridge to deliver medicine to a sick Pokémon. But the gang wouldn't let them cross. The leader of the gang sent out a Rock Pokémon called a Golem to battle Ash. Ash called on Charmander.

Charmander obeyed Ash's every command. First, Charmander hit Golem with an Ember Attack. Charmander sprayed Golem with a shower of fiery sparks.

Then Ash ordered Charmander to do a Flamethrower Attack. Charmander unleashed a stream of flame at Golem.

Then Ash called for a Fire Spin. Charmander caused the flame to spin around and around until it became a spiral. The whirling flame surrounded Golem. The Rock Pokémon became a rolling ball of fire. Golem slammed into the bike gang.

Charmander had taken them all out in one attack.

Ash was so proud of Charmander after that battle. But that

wasn't the only thing that made Ash proud. Charmander was a great friend to Pikachu and the rest of Ash's Pokémon. When they weren't battling wild Pokémon or fighting Team Rocket, Charmander and Pikachu practiced their attacks or went exploring together. They even played games with each other. Ash was happy to see Charmander getting along so well with the other Pokémon. He was even happier to see Charmander's skill in Pokémon battles.

Ash called on Charmander again and again. The Fire Pokémon obeyed him every time. Ash used Charmander in battle so often that it wasn't long before the Pokémon evolved.

Ash would never forget that moment. It started when Ash called on Charmander to help him rescue a town from a squad of Exeggutor. A magician named Melvin had hypnotized the three-headed Pokémon. Now they were attacking the entire town. To stop them, Ash would have to wake them up.

Bulbasaur's vines couldn't do it. Squirtle's water couldn't do it. But Charmander blasted the Exeggutor with waves of fire. Charmander didn't give up. With a little help from Melvin, Charmander's fire power woke up the Exeggutor and stopped their attack.

After the battle, Charmander's body began to glow with white light. The light exploded, and a transformed Pokémon stood in Charmander's place — Charmeleon. Charmeleon was over a foot taller than Charmander. Its sharp claws were longer and sharper. Its tail flame was brighter and bigger. And Charmeleon was a deeper orange-red.

Ash thought his new Charmeleon was amazing.

"Charmeleon just might be my most powerful Pokémon," Ash told Misty and Brock. The three friends walked through the woods to a small town called Moss Green Village. "I can't wait to use Charmeleon in battle!"

Brock pulled an empty bag out of his knapsack. He looked inside and frowned. "Battles will have to wait until later," Brock said. "Our Potion and Antidote bag is empty. Without it, we'll have no way to heal our Pokémon during battle. We'd better stop and get supplies."

"And some food," Misty said. "I'm hungry!"

"Potions and Antidotes first," Brock said. "There's a cottage up ahead. It looks like a Pokémon pharmacy."

Ash, Misty, and Pikachu followed Brock through the open door of the pharmacy. Inside an elderly woman with gray hair was mixing herbs in a bowl. A young girl with short brown hair helped her.

"Excuse me, but we'd like to buy some Potions and Antidotes if you have them," Brock said.

"We're Pokémon trainers," Ash explained.

The girl brightened. "Pokémon trainers? Great! Then let's battle out back."

The girl ran through the back door.

Brock shrugged. "I guess you get your battle after all, Ash," he said.

They followed the girl outside to the yard. The girl stood next to a small Bug Pokémon. It looked like an orange spider with two red-and-yellow mushrooms on its back.

"I'm Cassandra," the girl said. "And this is my Paras."

"Pika!" Pikachu smiled and waved to Paras.

Frightened, Paras skittled behind Cassandra's legs.

"Your Paras doesn't look like much of a fighter," Ash remarked.

"You're right," Cassandra said. "But I need Paras to battle so it will evolve into a Parasect. Then I can use Parasect's mushroom to make a new potion. The potion will be able to heal Pokémon all over the world."

"That's a wonderful thing to do," Brock said admiringly.

"We'll help!" Ash said. "Pikachu, battle Paras. But go easy on it!"

Pikachu nodded. It aimed a tiny electric shock at Paras — barely a spark.

The spark was too weak to do damage to most Pokémon — but not Paras. The Pokémon rolled over onto its back.

"Don't give up now, Paras!" Cassandra cried.

Ash thought. "Maybe Charmeleon will have better luck," he said.

Ash threw a Poké Ball. "Charmeleon, go!"

A bright light flashed and Charmeleon appeared.

"Charmeleon, don't hurt Paras! Let it attack you," Ash commanded.

Charmeleon looked at Ash angrily.

"I don't think Charmeleon wants to lose," Brock said.

Brock was right. Charmeleon ignored Ash. It shot a blast of fire at Paras.

Paras tried to dodge out of the way, but it was scorched.

Ash couldn't believe it. Charmander had always listened to him.

And now Charmeleon was disobeying him!

"Charmeleon! Stop!" Ash yelled.

Charmeleon didn't listen. It kept hitting Paras with Fire Blasts. When Paras tried to run away, Charmeleon hit Paras with its tail.

"Pikachu!" Angry at Charmeleon, Pikachu shocked it with an electric charge.

Charmeleon fainted. Ash quickly opened a Poké Ball and called it back.

A weakened and terrified Paras ran off into the woods.

Ash turned to Cassandra.

"Sorry about that," he said sheepishly.

Brock shook his head. "Ash, you've got a real problem with Charmeleon!"

5

Charmeleon Saves the Day — Sort Of

Ash felt terrible about what had happened to Paras. He and his friends combed the woods for hours, looking for it.

I can't believe Charmeleon wouldn't obey me, Ash thought as he marched through the trees. *This has never happened to me before.*

Ash and his friends searched and searched. But they couldn't find Paras.

Cassandra sighed and sat down on a

rock. "Paras is never coming back," she wailed.

"I'm sorry, Cassandra," Ash said. "It's all my fault."

Suddenly, they all heard a clicking noise. Paras emerged from the trees. Behind it stood Jessie, James, and Meowth — Team Rocket!

"What are you creeps doing here?" Ash asked. "And what have you done with Paras?"

"We've just helped to train it," Jessie said sweetly. "Paras is ready to battle now."

James chuckled under his breath. "Little do those twerps know that we overheard Cassandra talking about her potion," he whispered to Meowth. "She'll be so grateful to us for helping Paras that she's sure to cut us in on the profits."

"We'll be million-aires!" Meowth said, its eyes gleaming.

Cassandra hugged Paras. "You look great," she said. "Are you really ready to battle?"

Paras nodded.

"You finally understand my dream!" Cassandra said. "You're ready to evolve into Parasect!"

"I won't let you down this time," Ash said. "Pikachu, are you ready to battle Paras? Go easy on it again."

"Pika!" Pikachu nodded and approached Paras. Paras pinched Pikachu's lightning-bolt tail with one of its pincers. Pikachu started to give it a shock — then thought twice. It fell to the ground and went to sleep.

"That's great! Paras wins!" Cassandra said.

Ash took out Charmeleon's Poké Ball.

I don't know what went wrong before, Ash thought. *I have to try again.*

"Charmeleon, go!" Ash called out.

Charmeleon appeared. Instead of taking a battle stance, it lay down and closed its eyes.

44

"I don't get it!" Ash said. "Charmander always did what I told it to do."

Brock put a hand on Ash's shoulder. "A higher-level Pokémon like Charmeleon needs to be with an experienced trainer," Brock explained. "If the trainer doesn't have enough experience, the Pokémon won't obey it."

Ash frowned.

Cassandra looked nervous. "Call it back! It's too strong!"

Ash opened the Poké Ball. "Charmeleon, return!"

Charmeleon turned to Ash and shot a burst of fire in his face. Then it turned around and shot a spiral of fire at Paras.

"Charmeleon, stop!" Ash cried.

"If Paras loses, we'll lose our millions," Jessie said.

"We've got to do something!" Jessie cried.

Meowth gave out a cheer. "You can do it, Paras!"

Team Rocket jumped up and down and cheered for the Pokémon.

The cheer made Paras confident. It looked ready to fight.

But Charmeleon turned and shot a powerful fire blast at Team Rocket. Jessie, James, and Meowth went flying through the air. The attack scared Paras. It ran away.

Charmeleon stomped after it. Soon Charmeleon had Paras cornered against a tree.

Paras closed its eyes. It stuck out one of its pincers.

Charmeleon walked right into the pincer. The sharp pincer pinched Charmeleon's stomach.

Charmeleon roared. It fell backward, knocked out by the unexpected attack.

"Paras! You did it!" Cassandra said happily.

Suddenly, Paras began to glow with white light. The light glowed brightly, then dimmed.

Paras had become Parasect. Its entire back was covered with one large mushroom.

"Now I can make my Pokémon healing potion!" Cassandra said. She hugged Parasect.

Charmeleon opened its eyes. It stood up and charged at Parasect.

"Charmeleon, stop!" Ash pleaded.

Charmeleon still wouldn't listen.

"Parasect! Use your Spore Attack!" Cassandra commanded.

Spores that looked like particles of yellow dust floated from Parasect's body. The spores floated through the air and covered Charmeleon. The Pokémon fell to the ground and began to sleep.

Ash quickly opened a Poké Ball and called Charmeleon back.

"Well, I guess everything turned out all right," Ash said. "Parasect evolved. And it was all because of Charmeleon — sort of."

"You got lucky this time," Brock said. "But you'd better be careful with Charmeleon from now on. If you can't control your Pokémon, you don't know what kind of trouble you'll get into!"

Quest for a Volcano Badge

Ash refused to believe that Brock was right about Charmeleon. He was sure the Pokémon would obey him the next time he called on it.

Ash couldn't have been more wrong.

The last time Ash called on Charmeleon was when he was faced with a bunch of prehistoric Pokémon. Ash was trapped in a cave with a Kabuto, a Kabutops, an Omanyte, and an Omastar. Pikachu tried to battle the Pokémon, but there were too many. So Ash called on Charmeleon to help.

Charmeleon took a nap.

Ash couldn't believe it. He begged Charmeleon to fight, but it wouldn't listen.

The battle woke up a combination Rock and Flying Pokémon — an Aerodactyl. With its leathery wings and sharp claws, it was a dangerous creature.

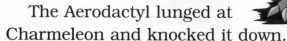

The Aerodactyl lunged at Charmeleon and knocked it down.

Charmeleon got angry.

Then it did something amazing.

There was an explosion of yellow fire around Charmeleon. When the fire cleared, Charizard stood in its place.

Charmeleon had evolved on purpose! Just so it could beat Aerodactyl and win. And that's just what it did.

Compared to its previous forms, Charizard was huge. It looked like a large, orange dragon. The fire on the end of

its tail burned with more intensity than ever before. And Ash had never seen a Flamethrower attack like Charizard's.

Ash was proud to have such a strong Pokémon on his team.

But Charmeleon had never listened to Ash. Would Charizard?

Ash wasn't sure.

For a while, Ash was afraid to call on Charizard.

But when Ash traveled to Cinnabar Island to battle the Gym Leader there for his Volcano Badge, he knew Charizard would be useful.

Ash, Brock, and Misty had traveled to Cinnabar Island in search of the legendary gym there. They finally found the hidden gym — inside an active volcano!

Now Ash faced Blaine, the Gym Leader of Cinnabar Island. The battle area was a platform stretched out over a pit of bubbling, steaming lava. Above them, Ash could see a circle of blue sky through the opening of the volcano.

Blaine loved his Fire Pokémon. He also loved to think up riddles.

"Here's a riddle for you, Ash," Blaine called out. "Where's one place that a firefighter can never win?"

"A firefighter?" Ash wondered. "I don't know."

But Misty got it. "In a volcano!" Misty cried.

"That's right!" Blaine said. "A firefighter could never win a battle against the heat and flames in this volcano. And you won't win your battle either!"

"We'll see about that!" Ash responded.

"Be careful, Ash," Brock called from the sidelines. "He must raise some awesome Fire Pokémon in this volcano!"

"I can handle it," Ash called back.

Blaine's eyes gleamed. "We'll see about that," he said. He threw a Poké Ball out onto the battle area. "Go, Ninetales!"

A white Pokémon that looked like a fox appeared. Ninetales had nine bushy tales.

53

Ash checked his Pokédex before making a decision about which Pokémon to use.

"Ninetales, the Fox Pokémon, is the evolved form of the Fire Pokémon, Vulpix," Dexter said.

"I knew he'd choose a Fire Type!" Ash said. "Big mistake!"

Ash picked a Poké Ball from his belt and threw it onto the gym floor. "Go, Squirtle!" he called.

Squirtle appeared and faced Ninetales.

"Go, Ninetales!" Blaine ordered. "Fire Spin now!"

"Fire Spin is Ninetales's most powerful attack!" Brock said.

Ninetales shot a stream of fire from its mouth. The fire flew toward Squirtle.

"Squirtle, Water Gun now!" Ash commanded.

Squirtle shot a strong stream of water

from its mouth. The water blast collided with the wall of flame.

It wasn't strong enough to put out the fire.

Quickly, Squirtle pulled its head, arms, and legs inside its shell. The fire hit the shell with full force. Squirtle's scorched shell clattered to the gym floor.

"Squirtle! You can do it. Don't give up now!" Ash shouted.

Squirtle poked its head out of its shell, but it was too weak to respond.

Blaine laughed. "Choosing a Pokémon is more than selecting the right type. It takes wisdom to win a gym battle!"

Ash knew Blaine was right. He thought hard. He didn't have a Water Pokémon strong enough to take out Ninetales. If only he had a Fire Pokémon stronger than Ninetales. That would work.

But he did.

Charizard.

In the heat of the battle, Ash didn't think twice.

"I'll fight Fire with Fire!" he yelled. "Charizard, I choose you!"

Charizard appeared on the gym floor. It stomped its feet and flapped its big wings.

Blaine nodded, impressed. "So you've chosen a Charizard. I can handle that!" He opened a Poké Ball. "Return, Ninetails!"

Blaine threw another ball. "Go, Rhydon!"

Ash checked Dexter as the large, gray Pokémon appeared on the gym floor.

"Rhydon, the evolved form of Rhyhorn," Dexter said. "It is known as the Drill Pokémon. Its large horn gives it formidable attack power. It is a combination Ground and Rock Pokémon."

Ash knew Blaine was smart. A Ground and Rock Pokémon could withstand Fire Attacks. But Charizard was still more powerful. Ash knew it could win.

"Give it all you've got, Charizard!" Ash yelled.

Charizard absently scratched behind its ear.

"Charizard is disobeying Ash!" Misty cried. "Just like Charmeleon."

Ash groaned. "Please, Charizard! I'm begging you!"

Charizard ignored Ash. The Pokémon didn't budge.

"Rhydon! Horn Drill!" Blaine ordered.

Rhydon lowered its head. Its horn began to spin like a drill. Rhydon charged at Charizard.

Charizard lazily opened an eye. It moved out of the way of the attack.

Then Charizard flew up to an outcropping on the volcano wall. It closed its eyes and fell asleep.

"Charizard has left the ring!" Blaine called out. "The victory goes to Rhydon!"

Ash turned to Pikachu. "It's up to you now!" he said.

Pikachu hopped out onto the floor. It quickly took care of Rhydon with a lightning bolt aimed at its horn. The horn acted as a lightning rod. Electricity surged through Rhydon's body, and it fell to the ground.

"Not bad," Blaine said. "But you haven't seen my best Pokémon."

The lava under the battle platform began to bubble and gurgle. A figure emerged from the lava.

This Pokémon looked like it was made of flame. It had sharp spikes down its back.

"Magmar!" Blaine said proudly.

Magmar leaped onto the battle platform.

"Magmar, the spit-fire Pokémon," Dexter said. "Its body is like a furnace, making Magmar a living inferno. It has been discovered only near active volcanoes."

Ash paled. This Pokémon sounded tough to beat.

"Magmar! Fire Punch!" Blaine commanded.

Magmar formed its hands into flaming fists and began aiming fiery punches at Pikachu. Pikachu dodged the punches, but Magmar kept attacking. Pikachu moved back farther and farther — to the edge of the platform.

"Magmar! Fire Blast!" yelled Blaine.

"Ash," Brock called out in a panicked voice. "That attack is way too powerful for Pikachu!"

"Pikachu can handle it!" Ash called back.

Magmar faced Pikachu and shot out a giant flame in the shape of a star. The star flame came at Pikachu with lightning speed. Pikachu jumped off the platform. It grabbed hold of the edge and dangled over the boiling lava.

"Ash! You've got to call back Pikachu!" Brock cried.

Ash knew Brock was right. It was too dangerous.

"Pikachu, I've got you!" Ash cried. He jumped onto the platform and pulled Pikachu to safety.

"I congratulate you for making a wise

decision," Blaine said. "If you had been foolish enough to continue the match, you definitely would have been disqualified as a Pokémon trainer."

Then Blaine grinned. "Anyway, it looks like you won't be getting your Volcano Badge today!"

Ash groaned. He couldn't believe he had lost.

And it was all Charizard's fault!

7

A Hot Time in the Volcano

"Pika pi," Pikachu said sadly.

Ash was giving Pikachu a bath in one of the hot springs outside of the volcano.

"You don't have to apologize, Pikachu," Ash said. "You did your best. Besides, I'm not leaving this island until I beat Blaine and Magmar — and get that badge!"

Pikachu smiled. *"Pikachu!"*

Misty shook her head. "I can't believe you still want to battle Magmar," she said. "Its Fire Blast is way too strong!"

"If Charizard would battle, I know I'd win," Ash protested.

Misty laughed. "I think there's a better chance of this volcano freezing than Charizard ever obeying you!"

Ash was about to shoot back a reply when a loud rumbling noise filled the air.

"What was that?" Ash asked. The ground around him began to shake.

Blaine ran up. "Something's happening down in the gym. I'm going to check it out."

Ash ran after him. "We'll help!"

Ash, Misty, Brock, and Pikachu followed Blaine as he entered the volcano and descended to the gym floor.

The group let out a gasp. The walls around them were covered with ice!

"Uh, Ash, forget about what I said before," Misty said.

"Ice in a volcano," Blaine said. "That's what I call *freezer* burn."

"Maybe you'd better *cool* it with the jokes," Ash said. "We need to figure out how this happened."

Three figures emerged from behind a rock.

They were Jessie, James, and Meowth. They each wore a padded suit. Jessie and James carried two long, wide tubes with triggers.

"Freeze, wimp!" Jessie yelled.

"You're interrupting our plan," James said. "With these freezing machines, we're going to capture Magmar."

"Then we'll use Magmar to beat Pikachu!" Meowth said.

Angry, Magmar rose from the lava and faced Team Rocket. Jessie and James aimed their freezing machines at the Pokémon.

"We'll get you this time!" Jessie cried.

They aimed the tubes at Magmar and shot two blasts of freezing-cold air. Magmar dodged the blasts. The air hit a rock sticking out from the volcano wall and covered it with ice.

"We've got to stop them!" Blaine cried. "Freezing all this hot rock could set off a giant chain reaction deep inside the volcano."

The icy rock began to tremble. With a loud crack the rock broke from the wall and crashed onto the gym floor.

"I knew it! The ice is cooling off the rock. It's cracking apart!" Blaine said. "Soon lava will flow through the cracks in the rock. The surge will cause a huge volcanic eruption!"

Team Rocket ignored Blaine's warnings. They shot blast after freezing blast at Magmar. Each blast covered the rocks and walls of the volcano with ice.

"How can we stop them?" Ash asked.

"I think it's too late for that," Brock said. "Look!"

All around the volcano, rocks were cracking and shattering. Four chains attached Blaine's gym platform to the volcano walls. The rocks around these chains were beginning to crack, too. The chains broke off the walls. The platform splashed into the hot lava below.

"My gym!" Blaine cried. "It's ruined!"

Team Rocket stood on a circular pillar of rock that rose up from the lava pit. As the battle platform fell, the surge sent the rock shooting up into the air. The rock — and Team Rocket — shot through the top of the volcano.

"It looks like Team Rocket is blasting off again!" Team Rocket cried as they flew through the air.

"That takes care of Team Rocket," Ash said. "But what about the volcano?"

Blaine looked panicked. "Lava is starting to burst through the cracks. I'm afraid it's only a matter of minutes until the volcano

blows." He looked thoughtful, then his face lit up. "Magmar! If you pile up rocks in the crater, it might be enough to block the lava flow!"

Magmar nodded and began picking up rocks and throwing them into the crater. Pikachu wanted to help, too. It picked up a rock and started to walk to the edge of the lava pit.

"Wait, Pikachu!" Blaine shouted. "Only a Fire Pokémon can withstand the heat from that lava."

"A Fire Pokémon!" Ash said. He threw a Poké Ball. "Charizard, I choose you!"

Charizard appeared.

"Charizard, help Magmar to block the crater and stop the lava flow now!" Ash ordered.

Charizard turned its back on Ash.

Ash couldn't believe it. "Charizard, you have to listen to me sometime!"

Charizard ignored Ash. Meanwhile, Magmar had not stopped working. The Fire Pokémon piled rock after rock into the crater.

It just wasn't enough. Every time the pile looked solid, lava came crashing through.

Magmar tried to go faster and faster. It wouldn't give up.

Charizard pretended to sleep. But it watched Magmar with one eye open.

Magmar kept piling rocks into the crater. It looked weak and exhausted. But it didn't slow down.

Charizard opened the other eye. It craned its neck and watched Magmar.

Charizard stood up. It stretched its wings. Then it walked over, picked up a rock, and began to help Magmar.

"Charizard must be impressed by Magmar," Misty said. "It wants to help now."

"This is great!" Blaine cried. "Two Pokémon are much more powerful than one!"

"Right!" Brock said. "Rock Pokémon can take the heat, too. Onix and Geodude, go!"

Onix looked like a giant snake made of rock. Geodude looked like a boulder with two strong arms. The two Pokémon began

to help Magmar and Charizard pile rocks onto the crater.

Misty called on Starmie to keep them cool while they worked. Ash called on Squirtle to do the same.

The Pokémon worked together to pile the rocks. After each trip back and forth from the lava pit, Squirtle and Starmie cooled them down with a squirt of water.

The cooling water even made it possible for Pikachu to help, too.

"Now, that's what I call teamwork!" Ash said.

It wasn't long before enough rocks were piled in the crater to keep the lava from exploding. The rocky walls stopped shaking and cracking.

The danger was over!

"I don't know how to thank you, Ash," Blaine said. "Perhaps if I give you —"

"Are you going to give me my Volcano Badge now?" Ash asked.

Blaine laughed in surprise. "No, I was about to say that I'll give you another chance to *battle* me for your Volcano Badge."

Ash blushed a little.

"Okay," he said. He turned to Pikachu. Pikachu looked exhausted. "Are you ready to battle Magmar?" Ash asked.

Before Pikachu could answer, Charizard stepped up and faced Ash. It stomped its feet and stared at Magmar.

"Charizard? Are you saying you want to battle Magmar?" Ash asked.

Charizard nodded.

Ash couldn't believe it. Charizard was finally going to listen to him!

8

Charizard vs. Magmar

Charizard flexed its muscles, eager to battle.

"The gym floor is destroyed," Blaine said. "We'll have to hold the battle somewhere else."

Ash felt relieved. It wasn't easy battling on top of a lava pit!

"I know the perfect place," Blaine said. "There's another lava pit not far from here, on the outside of the volcano, near the top."

Ash groaned but he didn't object. After all, Charizard was on his side now. How could he lose?

Misty looked worried as they climbed up the volcano. "Don't get your hopes up with Charizard," she warned. "I don't think Charizard is doing this to please you."

Brock agreed.

"What do you mean?" Ash asked.

"I think Charizard saw how strong Magmar was," Brock said. "Charizard wants to see if it can beat Magmar. It wants to test itself."

"You might be right," Ash said. "But I just know Charizard won't let me down this time."

Soon they reached the lava pit. Inside the circular pit, reddish-orange lava bubbled and boiled. Tall stone pillars rose out of the lava, dotting the pit. Ash thought it looked like the pit could be crossed by jumping from one pillar to the next — although he didn't think he'd ever want to try it.

Blaine and Magmar walked around the

edge of the pit and faced Ash and Charizard from the other side.

Ash turned to Charizard. "All right, Charizard," Ash said. "We're ready to — hey!"

Charizard didn't wait for Ash's instructions. It jumped from one pillar to another in an effort to reach Magmar.

"I told you, Ash!" Misty called out.

Charizard stopped a few yards away from Magmar. It attacked the Fire Pokémon with a Flamethrower.

Magmar countered with another Flamethrower. A stream of fire shot from each Pokémon. The fire streams met, creating a huge explosion.

The explosion rocked the lava pit. The vibrations shook both Magmar and Charizard.

Magmar recovered first.

"Magmar, Fire Blast now!" Blaine called out.

Magmar shot a Fire Blast shaped like a giant, flaming star — the same attack it had used against Pikachu.

74

The star of fire raced toward Charizard.
The Pokémon held out its two hands and
stopped the Fire Blast in midair.

Charizard pushed with all its might. It
hurled the blast right back at Magmar.

Magmar absorbed the blast without
much damage. It glared angrily at
Charizard.

Magmar leaped across the lava pit and
landed on Charizard's pillar. Charizard

teetered back and forth.

Charizard fell off the pillar!

Ash gasped. He didn't know if Charizard could withstand the searing heat of the lava pit.

But Charizard reacted quickly. It flapped its wings and flew high into the sky above the volcano. Then it zoomed back down, aiming right for Magmar. Charizard knocked Magmar off the pillar.

Charizard stood on the pillar and proudly roared.

Magmar climbed out of the lava, unhurt.

That makes sense, Ash thought. *After all, Magmar lives in the volcano. The boiling lava can't hurt it.*

Magmar stood on the pillar in front of Charizard and faced its opponent.

The two Pokémon battled hand to hand. Charizard pushed Magmar off the pillar again. Charizard smiled.

But Magmar wasn't out of the battle yet. It climbed up the pillar, right behind Charizard. Then it grabbed Charizard's tail.

The attack caught Charizard by surprise. Magmar pulled with all its might.

Ash realized what it was trying to do. Magmar wanted to pull Charizard into the lava.

"It's against the rules for Magmar to pull Charizard into the volcano!" Ash cried.

"Magmar isn't cheating," Blaine called out. "You agreed to use the volcano for our Pokémon battle. Using the characteristics

of the battlefield to your advantage is the key to winning!"

Ash cringed. He looked out into the pit. Magmar had a good grip on Charizard. He pulled . . .

. . . and Magmar and Charizard both toppled into the boiling lava!

Ash looked down into the pit. All he could see was bubbling, steaming lava.

"Charizard!" Ash cried, his voice choking.

Suddenly the lava began to bubble faster. Charizard flew out of the lava — with Magmar on its back!

"Charizard! Show Magmar your Aerial Submission Attack!" Ash called out.

Charizard spun around in midair, creating a whirlwind. Magmar grew dizzy.

Ash turned to Blaine. "If Magmar can use the volcano, Charizard can use the sky! That's part of the battlefield, too."

Blaine just scowled.

"Charizard! Seismic Toss!" Ash called.

Now Charizard flew in circles. He flew and flew, gaining speed with each circle.

Finally the force of the speed sent Magmar flying off Charizard's back.

Magmar fell down into the lava pit and disappeared into the lava.

Ash watched the pit, breathless. Was this the end of the match?

Without warning, the lava exploded in a mass of liquid flame. Magmar burst through the lava and landed on a pillar. It glared at Charizard, ready to attack.

Then it fainted!

"Magmar just couldn't recover from the Seismic Toss," Brock remarked.

Blaine sighed, then smiled. He walked along the edge of the pit and faced Ash.

"Congratulations, Ash. Charizard wins," he said. "And now I have one last riddle for you: What is it that is always red, but has no words?"

Ash was stumped.

Blaine held open his hand. A red badge glowed in his palm.

"The answer is a Volcano Badge," Blaine said. "It's *red*, but it has no words. And now it's yours." He handed Ash the badge.

"Thanks, Blaine," Ash said. "I couldn't have done it without Charizard."

Ash opened a Poké Ball. "Good work, Charizard. Now, return!"

Charizard replied with a Fire Blast — aimed right at Ash.

"Sorry, Ash," Brock said. "I guess we can't expect Charizard to ever change."

"That's what you think," Ash said confidently. "I know Charizard will learn to obey someday. I just know it!"

9

Back at the Stadium ...

Charmander, the stray Pokémon, coming to Pikachu's rescue . . .

Charmeleon disobeying him for the first time . . .

Charizard helping him win his Volcano Badge . . .

These thoughts and more raced through Ash's mind as he faced Richie in the Pokémon League battle arena.

I know Charizard will learn to obey some-day, Ash thought. *I just know it.*

Ash held Charizard's Poké Ball high over

his head. He really wanted to choose Charizard to battle.

He knew that Charizard could easily beat Richie's Charmander, Zippo.

But what if Charizard didn't obey him? That would be a disaster.

"Don't do it, Ash!" Misty called from the stands. "Choosing Charizard is a big mistake!"

"Think about your choice carefully, Ash!" Brock warned.

Ash didn't have much time to think. His Volcano Badge victory was fresh in his mind. Charizard was so amazing in that battle.

Charizard and I have been through so much together, Ash thought. *When it sees how important this match is, it will obey me.*

Ash made up his mind.

"Charizard, go!" Ash yelled. He threw the Poké Ball out into the arena.

The Fire Pokémon looked at Ash, annoyed, and folded its arms.

"I'm begging you. Please battle, Charizard!" Ash pleaded.

Charizard didn't respond. But behind it, Richie's Charmander, Zippo, ran in for the attack. It shot a blast of fire at Charizard's body.

Charizard grunted and turned around. The Fire Blast wasn't powerful enough to hurt it. But Charizard was angry.

Charizard stomped after Zippo. It shot a huge Fire Blast at the small Charmander. Zippo ran as fast as it could to the other end of the field.

"Charizard is too high-level for Zippo to handle," the announcer blared. "Zippo can't do a thing against Charizard!"

Richie frowned. "Return, Zippo!" he commanded.

Ash cheered. "We did it! Good work, Charizard! You're finally listening to me!"

"Not so fast," Richie called out. "I haven't lost yet. I can still choose one more Pokémon to battle Charizard."

Ash knew he was right. They were both allowed to use three Pokémon in the battle. Now they were each down to one.

But which Pokémon would Richie choose?

"Leon! It's your turn!" Richie cried. He threw a Poké Ball, and a small yellow Pokémon appeared in the arena.

A Pikachu!

"What's this?" the announcer said. "Richie has sent his Pikachu to face a Charizard? Does it have a chance?"

Ash was a little worried. He knew what a Pikachu could do.

"Be careful, Charizard," he warned. "This won't be as easy as it looks."

Leon didn't waste time. Sparks flew from its red cheeks. It ran at Charizard. The sparks hit Charizard's belly.

Charizard stomped its feet angrily and flapped its wings. The gust of wind blew the Pikachu back to the other end of the battle arena.

Pleased, Charizard blew smoke out of its nostrils.

Then it yawned.

Charizard reclined on the ground. It scratched its belly.

"What's this?" the announcer cried. "Ash's Charizard is taking a nap!"

Ash groaned. "Charizard, what are you doing? There's a battle going on here!"

Charizard snorted and ignored Ash.

This can't be happening! Ash thought. "Battle, Charizard! Please listen to me! We've been through so much together. You can't let me down now!"

Charizard didn't move. The large crowd began to grow angry. Ash could hear their taunts and jeers.

"We came here to see a Pokémon battle!"

"Get serious!"

In the stands, Ash's mom turned to

Professor Oak. "What's happening?" she asked.

"Charizard may have thought that Richie's Charmander, being a Fire Pokémon, was a worthy opponent," Professor Oak explained. "But I don't think it wants to bother fighting a little Pikachu."

Back on the field, Charizard snored away.

The judge walked out onto the battle area. "Charizard is refusing to battle. Piakchu wins. The victory in this match goes to Richie!"

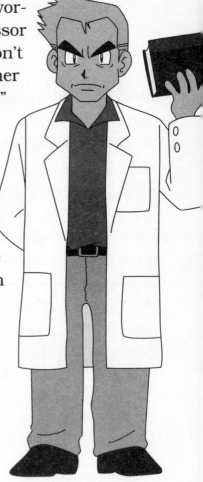

10

A New Dream

"Return, Charizard!" Ash called angrily. The combination Fire and Flying Pokémon vanished inside its Poké Ball.

Ash turned and faced Richie. Richie smiled and waved at the cheering crowd.

I lost, Ash thought. *I really lost. I won't be entering the Pokémon League. And the next tournament is a whole year from now.*

Ash wanted to run out of the stadium. He felt like crying.

But a tiny voice inside Ash kept him on the field.

I will be a Pokémon Master someday, Ash

told himself. *And a real Pokémon Master wouldn't cry or run away.*

Ash walked up to Richie and extended his hand.

"Congratulations, Richie," Ash said.

Richie shook Ash's hand and smiled. "Thanks, Ash. You were a tough opponent."

Ash nodded.

"Pika pi!" Pikachu ran up to Ash and jumped into his arms.

"Thanks, Pikachu," Ash said. "I'm glad you still believe in me."

Ash walked over to the stands.

Misty, Brock, Professor Oak, and his mom were waiting for him.

"You did a fine job," Professor Oak told him. "You have nothing to be ashamed of."

"I'm really proud of you, Ash," his mom said.

Ash sighed. "I know I have a long way to go before becoming a Pokémon Master. But I'm not going to give up. I'm going to keep gaining experience until there's no one better than I am."

Ash turned to Misty and Brock. "Are you guys still with me?"

Brock nodded. "Sure, Ash."

Misty smiled. "Of course, Ash. You still owe me a bike, remember?"

"Pikachu!" Pikachu hugged Ash, sending a tiny shock through his body.

Ash laughed. "That settles it, then," he said. "I'm going to be the greatest Pokémon Master in the world. I won't let anything stop me!"

Ash looked up at the giant flame that burned in a torch over the stadium.

He knew that becoming a Pokémon Master would be the best thing — and maybe the hardest thing — he'd ever do.

And he couldn't wait to continue his journey!

HEY, KIDS!
ENTER THE PIKACHU PEEKABOO CONTEST!

Count the number of times you see this Pikachu image in this book and enter to win valuable Pokémon Prizes.

Official Rules:

1. NO PURCHASE NECESSARY. To enter, complete this official entry coupon or hand print your name, address, birthdate and telephone number, and answer to the contest question on a 3" x 5" card and mail by 3/15/00 to: PIKACHU PEEKABOO! Contest, c/o Scholastic Inc., P.O. Box 7500, Jefferson City, MO 65101.

2. Contest open to residents of the USA no older than 15 as of 12/31/00, except employees of Scholastic Inc., its respective affiliates, subsidiaries, respective advertising, promotion, and fulfillment agencies, and immediate families. Contest is void where prohibited by law.

3. Except where prohibited, by accepting the prize, winner consents to the use of his/her name, age, entry, and/or likeness by sponsors for publicity purposes without further notice or compensation.

4. Winners will be judged by Scholastic Inc., whose decision is final, based on their answers. Only one prize per winner. All winners will be selected on or about 4/01/00, by Scholastic Inc., whose decision is final. Odds of winning are dependent on the number of entries received. Winners and their legal guardians will be required to sign and return an affidavit of eligibility and liability release within 14 days of notification, or the prize will be forfeited.

5. Prizes: **Grand Prize:** A set of Pokémon video games. (Estimated retail value: $200) **1st Prize:** 25 First Prize winners will receive a Pokémon home video. (Estimated retail value: $25). **2nd Prize:** 50 Second Prize winners will receive a Pokémon bag. (Estimated retail value $20). **3rd Prize:** 100 Third Prize winners will receive a Pokémon key chain. (Estimated retail value: $10) No substitution or transfer of prize allowed, except by sponsor due to prize unavailability.

6. Prizes are non-transferable, not returnable, and cannot be sold or redeemed for cash. No substitutions allowed. Taxes on prizes are the responsibility of the winner. By accepting the prize, winner agrees that Scholastic Inc. and its respective officers, directors, agents and employees will have no liability or responsibility for any injuries, losses or damages of any kind resulting from the acceptance, possession or use of any prize and they will be held harmless against any claims of any kind resulting from the acceptance, possession or use of any prize and they will be held harmless against any claims of any kind resulting from the prizes awarded.

7. For list of winners, send a self-addressed stamped envelope after 3/15/00 to: PIKACHU PEEKABOO! Contest WINNERS, c/o Scholastic Inc., P.O. Box 7500, 2931 East McCarty Street, Jefferson City, MO 64102.

CONTEST QUESTION
How many times does the Pikachu shown above appear in this book?_____

Name_____ Birth date_____

Address_____

City_____ State_____ Zip_____